FOCUS ON THE FAMILY PRESENTS

Swept into the Sea

BOOK 26

CHRIS BRACK AND SHEILA SEIFERT
ILLUSTRATIONS BY SERGIO CARIELLO

FOCUS
ON THE FAMILY.

A Focus on the Family Resource
Published by Tyndale House Publishers

This book is dedicated to:

C.B. – Breña, Ryder, Emily, Carter, Katie, Joey, Beau, Mason, Norah, and Natalie

S.S. – Beverly Johnson for her inspiration and love of family

Swept into the Sea

© 2020 Focus on the Family. All rights reserved.

A Focus on the Family book published by Tyndale House Publishers, Carol Stream, Illinois 60188.

The Imagination Station, Adventures in Odyssey, and *Focus on the Family,* along with their accompanying logos and designs, are federally registered trademarks of Focus on the Family, 8605 Explorer Drive, Colorado Springs, CO 80920.

TYNDALE and Tyndale's quill logo are registered trademarks of Tyndale House Publishers.

All Scripture quotations have been taken from *The Holy Bible, English Standard Version.* Copyright © 2001 by Crossway Bibles, a publishing ministry of Good News Publishers. Used by permission. All rights reserved.

Cover design by Michael Heath | Magnus Creative

For Library of Congress Cataloging-in-Publication Data for this title, visit http://www.loc.gov/help/contact-general.html.

For manufacturing information regarding this product, please call 1-800-323-9400.

For information about special discounts for bulk purchases, please contact Tyndale House Publishers at csresponse@tyndale.com, or call 1-800-323-9400.

Printed in the United States of America

ISBN: 978-1-64607-000-8

26 25 24 23 22 21 20
7   6   5   4   3   2   1

Contents

Contents

Prologue

In the last adventure, *Poison at the Pump*, Patrick and Beth learned more about the Imagination Station. The Model T car has a bubbling mixture in its engine. The bubbling mixture is a blend of three liquids.

The liquid is in a glass container. But the container was only half full.

Mr. Whittaker, the Imagination Station's inventor, wanted to fill up the container.

The cousins would go on an adventure to search for the liquids.

Whit gave the cousins a pocket-sized black box with a wand. On the top of the box was a light that looked like a button.

Whit told the cousins to dip the wand in liquids. The right liquid for the Imagination Station would turn the button green.

The cousins stepped into the Imagination Station.

But Whit noticed the container with the liquid was cracked. Drops were trickling out.

Whit said that a trip in the Imagination Station was too dangerous.

Patrick started to get out. But his elbow accidentally hit the red button on the steering wheel.

Beth and Patrick's adventure began.

The Imagination Station took the cousins to London during a time of great sickness in 1854. Here is how that adventure ended.

Patrick stuck the wand into a gray-blue oil. The button on Whit's gadget turned green.

"This is it!" Beth said.

Patrick whooped. He heard the hum of the Imagination Station. It was a welcome sound. The Model T appeared.

"I'm so glad to see the Imagination Station," Patrick said. "I thought we might be stuck here.

I was afraid too much of its power source had leaked."

"Me too," Beth said. "But now we can go home."

Patrick hopped into the passenger seat.

Beth slid into the driver's seat.

Patrick found the compartment on the passenger side. He placed the oil inside. Then he noticed a keyhole next to the compartment.

Patrick took the small key out of his pocket. It fit the lock perfectly. Patrick turned the key.

A sliding panel moved to cover the compartment. Then the panel opened. The container full of oil was no longer there. The oil was now inside the Imagination Station.

Beth put on her seat belt. "Ready?" she asked.

Patrick left the key in the lock. He buckled his seat belt. Patrick thought he might have the great sickness. He couldn't wait for the

Imagination Station to cure him. He couldn't wait to go home.

Beth hit the big red button.

The Model T sprayed them with a fine mist.

"What's happening?" Beth asked.

Patrick laughed. "Maybe it found the cholera germ on me. No germs are leaving with us," he said.

The Imagination Station made a loud squeak. Then metal scraped against metal.

Something didn't feel right to Patrick. He heard the sound of glass shattering and looked at Beth.

"There's that smell again," Beth said.

Patrick smelled it too. There was the scent of apricots, lemons, pears, and oranges.

The fine mist grew into a heavier spray. Drops of water began to rain on the inside of the Model T.

Then everything went black.

The Storm

It's a night without stars, Beth thought.

A shadowy form moved past the driver's-side window of the Imagination Station. Then it melted into the darkness.

"This isn't Whit's End," Beth said.

Icy cold water covered her feet and slowly climbed up her ankles.

"We must have landed in a river," Patrick said. "Or we're in a flood."

"Maybe. But something's out there," Beth said. "I saw it move."

"What was it?" Patrick asked.

"I don't know," she said. "I couldn't tell. It was too dark."

The Imagination Station shook as if it were a baby's rattle.

Beth fell against the driver's-side door. It flung open.

Splash!

Beth landed in a puddle on a hard, wooden surface. "Ow!" she said. The wood had a musty smell. "Patrick?" Her words were almost drowned out by a rumble of thunder.

Large raindrops fell from the sky and drenched her.

"I'm here," Patrick said.

Beth heard his footsteps splash on the wood. He slid around the front corner of the Model T.

"Whoa!" he said. His feet slipped out from under him. He landed with a thud.

"Are you okay?" she asked.

"I think so," he said. He rubbed his arm.

The Imagination Station flickered. Then it disappeared.

Beth felt a rocking motion. She had felt this type of movement before on another adventure. They had to be on the deck of a ship.

The ship creaked.

This must be an old wooden ship, Beth thought.

Crates and barrels were stacked everywhere on the deck. They kept Beth from seeing much of the ship. Canvas covered the wooden crates. The fabric was tied on with thick ropes. The edges of the canvas flapped in the wind.

Beth stood. Her feet were cold. She looked down. She was wearing sandals. Her feet were covered with bits of seaweed.

Patrick stood also.

Beth said, "Maybe we're sailors."

Patrick looked at their clothes. "We're dressed like people in Bible times," he said.

Beth looked at Patrick through the rain. He wore a soggy, tan tunic that stopped at his knees. A rope belt was around his waist. A leather pouch hung from it. He looked like he had stepped out of a Sunday school lesson.

Lightning lit the sky.

Beth looked down. Her tan dress stopped at her sandals. The dress was wet and heavy. It felt like one of her itchy wool sweaters.

She touched her head. Her hair was in a tight braid. The end of the braid fell over her shoulder. Beth also had a rope belt with a pouch hanging from it.

"You're right," Beth said. "We are dressed like Bible-times people. We might be in a Bible story. I wonder which one."

Patrick put his hand into his pouch. He pulled out Whit's gadget and knelt down. Then Patrick dipped the wand into the water on the ship's deck.

Beth held her breath.

The light on the gadget did not turn green.

Beth sighed. "That would have been too easy," she said.

There was liquid all around them. But they needed the right liquid for the Imagination Station.

Patrick grunted. He put the gadget back

into his pouch. Then he pulled out a pair of green swimming goggles. They glowed in the dark. He put them on.

Beth laughed. The goggles looked out of place on the old ship.

Patrick took them off and put them back into his pouch. "What do you have?" he asked.

Beth pulled out a large bag of dried leaves. She opened the bag and took a leaf. It broke in half.

"Smells like peppermint," Patrick said.

"Strange," Beth said. She closed the bag. The Imagination Station had given them these gifts. Beth had no idea why.

"The goggles and the leaves will come in handy," Patrick said.

Beth nodded. The Imagination Station's gifts were always helpful. She put the bag of peppermint leaves back in her leather pouch.

"I wonder where this ship is going," Beth said.

"I don't know. But I hope it gets there soon," Patrick said. "The storm is really bad. Maybe we can ask someone."

"Like who? I haven't seen anyone," Beth said. She wondered if the shadowy figure counted as someone.

"It's a large ship. It must have a large crew and a captain," Patrick said. "Oh no!" He pointed behind her.

Beth looked over her shoulder.

A ten-foot wave was coming over the side of the ship. It was moving directly toward them.

Beth reached for Patrick's hand.

"Hold on tight," he said. He squeezed her hand.

The wave crashed into them. It pushed Beth off her feet and onto her back.

Patrick fell beside her.

They started sliding with the water.

Beth's free arm and shoulder slammed into

a crate. Then her arm scraped against a large wooden barrel.

Beth screamed. Her arm throbbed in pain. But she still grasped at every passing crate with her free hand. Her fingers slipped off each one.

Beth saw Patrick trying to stop also. He was using his legs to find footholds between objects. He kept slipping too.

The wave passed over the side of the ship.

Beth rubbed the salty water out of her eyes.

Another wave came over the side of the ship. And another. They weren't as large. But they were powerful.

The cousins kept sliding.

A small patch of deck was between the barrels and the railing. And she and Patrick were headed straight toward it.

Someone appeared on the other side of the

barrels. It was a man on his knees with folded hands.

Patrick yelled, "Watch out!"

Then the cousins slammed into him.

A Man of God

Patrick landed on Beth, and Beth landed on the stranger.

"Aughhh," the man said. His graying mustache and beard danced in the wind beneath his long nose.

Patrick used the ship's railing to pull himself up.

"I'm so sorry," Beth said. She rolled away from the stranger. Then she stood.

The waves were still coming. But the barrels shielded them. The rain continued to fall.

"Are you okay?" Patrick asked. He hoped they hadn't hurt the older man.

Patrick held out a hand to help the man up.

The stranger took Patrick's hand. But he used his own strength to stand.

The man had dark eyes. His wet, tan robe stopped at his ankles. A brown cloak went from his shoulders to his sandals. He looked like he was from Bible times too.

"Thank you," the man said. He didn't sound upset. His voice was kind. "You must have lost your footing."

"Yes," Beth said. "I thought we'd be thrown over the railing and into the sea."

"This storm threatens to pull all two hundred seventy-six of us into the sea," the stranger said. "But it hasn't taken even one yet."

"That's a lot of people!" Patrick said. "Where are they?"

The stranger pointed toward the center of the ship.

Patrick peeked over the top of a barrel. He could just make out the outlines of people. They were huddled together in large groups. They were trying to protect one another from the storm. Many people were sleeping.

"Why isn't everyone below deck?" Beth asked. "It would be safer there."

"Below deck is filled with grain," the man said. "People and cargo stay on the deck. You should know that by now. We've been fighting this storm for more than a day."

"I guess I'm a little confused," Beth said. "It's been a long night."

The stranger nodded, as if he agreed. "My midnight prayers have never ended like this before. But life is full of surprises. I don't think we've met," he said.

"My name is Patrick," Patrick said. "This is my cousin Beth."

"Hello," Beth said. "Thank you for stopping us."

"You are welcome," the man said. "But I didn't have a choice." He gave them a warm smile. "My name is Paul."

Paul looked at Beth oddly. "You're the first girl I've met onboard," he said. He leaned toward her. "That's quite a scrape on your arm."

Patrick turned toward his cousin.

Beth was holding her arm.

Patrick felt bruised from the waves and the hard, wooden deck. But he hadn't scraped against anything.

"Are you okay?" he asked.

"I cut my arm on something," Beth said. "It really hurts."

"Come with me," Paul said. "I'll take you to my friend Luke. He's a doctor."

Patrick and Beth followed Paul.

The waves kept coming.

Paul leaned with the ship and walked slowly through the crowds.

Patrick leaned too. *The waves won't knock me off my feet again*, he thought. Patrick started counting his steps. This ship was even larger than it looked at first.

Paul said, "Are you followers of the Way?"

"Which way?" Beth asked.

"There's only one Way. Let me tell you about my Lord," Paul said. "I am His servant. I once fought the Way and tried to harm followers of the Truth. But I saw a great light on the road to Damascus."

The name Damascus sounded familiar

to Patrick. *Where have I heard it before?* he wondered. Nothing came to mind.

Patrick returned to counting his steps. *Eighty-seven. Eighty-eight.*

"Luke? Aristarchus?" Paul called.

Patrick whispered to Beth, "This ship is almost the size of a football field."

Beth didn't look at him. She winced in pain.

Patrick watched Paul's friends. They came forward. Both young men wore tunics and cloaks like Paul.

"Luke, my friend Beth has hurt her arm," Paul said. "Would you look at it?"

"Of course," Luke said. "Come with me, Beth."

Patrick was surprised Beth went with him. Her arm must really hurt.

Suddenly the names made sense to him. *Paul. Damascus. Luke.*

Patrick knew who these people were. This man was Paul from the New Testament. He was part of the early church after Jesus returned to God the Father. Patrick felt excitement grow inside of him. Paul was one of his heroes of faith.

"I leave you in the hands of good friends," Paul said. "I must be off. I promised to help another new friend after my prayers." He gave a short wave and left.

Patrick wanted to follow Paul. But he knew he should wait for Beth. They'd find Paul together later. First, Luke had to patch up her arm.

"Hi, I'm Aristarchus," the man next to Patrick said.

He was about a foot taller than Patrick. His skin was very tan, and he had deep dimples. His mouth was turned up at the ends like he wanted to laugh.

"Aris Tar Kiss?" Patrick asked. What an odd first, middle, and last name.

The man laughed. "You can call me Aris," he said.

"Hi, Aris, my name is Patrick," Patrick said.

"Hello, Patrick," Aris said. "How do you come to be on this grain ship?"

"It's a long story," Patrick said. "I guess I'm here for the adventure. How about you?"

"I'm a prisoner," Aris said. "Many of us are."

Patrick looked at the men with shaggy beards around him. They were all huddled together. He was on a grain ship surrounded by prisoners!

And then a thought even worse worked into Patrick's mind.

Are Beth and I prisoners too? he wondered.

Paul's Doctor

Luke lifted Beth onto a crate. Then he swung a large cloth pouch off his shoulder. "First, I need to clean your wound," he said. He set the pouch next to her. Then he took out a cloth.

Beth bit her lip.

The cloth scraped against her skin. Tears welled in her eyes.

Luke said, "We don't want any wood slivers

in there." He reached into his medical pouch and pulled out tweezers.

Beth was surprised they had tweezers in Bible times.

Luke held Beth's arm gently. He started removing splinters from her scrape.

Beth tried not to pay attention to what Luke was doing. She looked straight ahead.

Stacked crates rose in front of her. This area was filled with furniture, barrels, and wooden boxes. The rain kept falling. But the crates, barrels, and boxes protected them from the wind.

Finally, Luke let go of her arm. "Now I'll put aloe oil on it," he said.

"Okay," Beth said. She hoped the aloe didn't sting. "I'm glad those crates block the waves."

Luke nodded. "They're the ship's cargo," he said. "The cargo helps block the wind." Luke dabbed oil on the long scrape.

"What's in all those crates?" Beth asked. The oil felt soothing.

"Some are filled with food. Others hold nails, linens, chains, and even swords," Luke said. "They also hold the belongings of the passengers." He took out a clean cloth and wrapped it around Beth's arm.

Beth smiled. "Thank you," she said. Then it dawned on her. Aloe oil might be what the Imagination Station needed.

Beth looked around for Patrick. He could dip the gadget's wand into it. Patrick was still by Paul's other friend. She would tell him about it later.

Luke picked up his medicine pouch. He slung it back over his shoulder.

Suddenly, wind swooshed down on Beth. Water splashed around her.

Why wasn't the cargo protecting them? she wondered.

A sailor was moving the crates in front of her.

Another was unstacking the crates beside her.

Suddenly, the crate she sat on moved.

Beth looked behind her. "What are you doing?" she yelled.

Two strong sailors were pulling her crate.

"All cargo must go overboard," a soldier said. "We avoided the sandbars of Syrtis by lowering the sea anchor. Now we need to lighten the ship."

"Would you take the child with it?" Luke yelled. A muscle in his jaw twitched. Luke reached out to Beth.

Beth grabbed Luke's hands and jumped off the wooden box.

The sailors ignored Luke. They kept pulling the crate toward the ship's edge.

A soldier rolled a barrel past them.

Luke and Beth moved out of his way.

Then the soldier lifted the barrel over the railing. He threw the barrel into the sea.

Another soldier bumped into Beth. He was tugging a wooden box to the edge of the ship.

"Excuse me," Beth said.

"Quiet, child," a passenger whispered. "They might throw us over next."

Beth hoped that wasn't true. But she shut her lips tightly.

A sailor reached for a small crate.

"Wait," Luke said. "My parchments are in that one."

The sailor ignored Luke.

Beth watched the sailor drop Luke's box into the sea.

Luke sighed. But then he said, "Better to

lose what doesn't matter than what does. I've heard Paul say that many times."

"Didn't your parchments matter?" Beth asked.

"To me they did. But not in comparison to my relationship with God," Luke said.

Beth realized something. Luke had just lost all his possessions. Everyone on this ship had too. But no one was complaining. Maybe this storm was worse than she thought.

The deck was colder without the crates. Beth shivered.

Luke took off his brown cloak. He wrapped it around Beth's shoulders.

The cloak was wet. But it was warm.

"Thank you," Beth said.

Sailors picked up a large crate by the ship's edge. They strained to toss it into the sea.

"They should toss that over," Luke said. He pointed to a large tree trunk on its side. It was rolling back and forth on the deck.

"What is that?" Beth asked.

"It's the mast. It held the mainsail," Luke said. "But the wind and waves broke it."

The mast looked like a huge telephone pole.

"What will you do without your things?" she asked.

"We'll have to start over in Rome," Luke said.

A sailor rolled another barrel past them.

Beth took a step closer to Luke. "This ship is headed to Rome?" she asked.

"Yes," Luke said. "Paul was arrested for preaching the gospel. He goes to Rome to stand trial."

"Why are you traveling on this ship?" she asked.

"I travel with Paul," Luke said. "I help him with his pains and illnesses."

"Is Paul sick?" Beth asked.

"Yes and no," Luke said. "Paul calls it a thorn in his flesh."

Beth touched her bandaged arm. "Does it hurt?" she asked. Rain dripped from her braid down her back.

"At times," Luke said. "Paul has asked God to remove it. But God hasn't yet."

Beth frowned.

"That isn't a bad thing. God did something better," Luke said. He stepped aside for soldiers to get to a crate behind him. "God became Paul's strength. Paul's weakness shows God's strength."

Beth shook her head. "That won't take Paul's pain away," she said.

"No, it won't," Luke said. "But it helps Paul keep preaching the gospel to anyone who will listen. And I will be by his side. I will write everything down. Then everyone will know how great God is."

Beth thought for a moment. Luke was a writer. Luke followed Paul. Her eyes opened wide. She was with Luke, the author of two books in the Bible.

But then Beth had an awful thought. "You've lost your parchments!" she said. They had been thrown into the sea. All his writings were gone.

"God will give me new parchment," Luke said. "He will give me the words to fill them."

Beth felt relieved. But then she stared at Luke's medical pouch. Would the soldiers toss that into the sea too? She hoped not. The Imagination Station might need Luke's aloe oil.

The Lifeboat

Patrick felt Aris shove him. "Watch out!" Aris yelled.

A barrel rolled by them.

"That was close," Aris said.

Patrick wondered why the soldiers and sailors treated everyone so poorly. He asked, "Is everyone in this area a prisoner?"

"No. You aren't," Aris said. "There are also

travelers, merchants, and off-duty soldiers and sailors."

"Why are you a prisoner?" he asked.

"Just like Paul," Aris said, "I tell people about Jesus."

"That's not a crime, is it?" Patrick asked.

"Some Jewish leaders think it is," Aris said. "Hopefully Caesar won't agree with them."

The ship creaked.

Patrick's brows knit together. "Is the ship strong enough to get through this storm?" he asked.

"I'm not certain. Maybe Luke could tell us. We might need to take it to the doc," Aris said.

Patrick laughed. Ships are tethered to a dock, and *doc* is short for the word *doctor.*

Aris laughed too.

Patrick looked

around. Most of the cargo had been thrown overboard.

Now Patrick could see Luke and Beth in the distance.

He saw a large Roman soldier near Beth. The soldier wore armor over his tunic. The man also wore a metal helmet.

"What is that soldier doing?" Patrick asked.

"He is guarding the prisoners," Aris said.

"Does Paul have a guard?" Patrick said.

"His guard is a Roman centurion named Julius," Aris said. "Julius trusts Paul. He lets Paul walk about freely."

Aris looked around. Then he said, "I'll bring you to your friend. I need to check on Paul. He tries to help everyone. But sometimes he needs help."

Patrick pointed. "I see Beth over there," he said. "Go help Paul. I'll be fine."

Patrick started to walk toward Beth.

Aris smiled and called out, "What's a sailor's least favorite color?"

Patrick turned back and shrugged.

"Maroon," Aris said.

Patrick laughed. Marooned sailors are stuck on an island without a boat. And maroon is a dark red color.

Patrick waved and left.

Patrick stepped around people standing. He moved carefully between resting sailors and soldiers.

How could they sleep in such a noisy storm? Patrick wondered.

A figure sat up and stretched as Patrick walked by. He seemed to be a few years older than Patrick. The teen wore a short skirt with sashes over his shoulders. He was dressed like a Roman sailor.

Patrick knew about Roman sailors. He had been in Rome on an earlier adventure.

Patrick stopped watching where he was going to see where Beth was. He stepped on something soft and lumpy.

A Roman soldier sat up. "I'm trying to sleep," he yelled. His thick black eyebrows formed a V on his forehead.

"I'm sorry," Patrick said.

"You're not as sorry as you will be," the soldier said. He stood. He was more than twice Patrick's size.

"Leave him alone, Demetrius," the young sailor said.

"Is he your friend, Marcus?" Demetrius asked. "Then I'll teach you both a lesson."

The boy jumped to his feet.

The soldier's hairy arms reached toward Patrick.

But Marcus grabbed Patrick first. He pulled Patrick away from the soldier. "Run!" he yelled.

Patrick took off after Marcus. He slipped and slid across the deck.

Marcus slipped also. They were running too fast.

"I know a place to hide," Marcus said. He pointed.

Patrick saw a small wooden lifeboat near the ship's railing. It was lashed to the deck.

Canvas was tied over the top of the lifeboat. The storm had loosened the ropes around the canvas. The cloth no longer completely covered the lifeboat.

"What's that doing here?" Patrick asked. He thought lifeboats were supposed to be on the outside of a ship.

"We were going to lose it in the storm," Marcus said. "We had to hoist it aboard."

A wave crashed over them.

Marcus dove under the canvas tarp.

Patrick did too. He landed in a puddle of freezing water.

"Yikes!" he yelled.

"Oooh! That's cold," Marcus said.

"Why was that soldier so mean?" Patrick asked.

Marcus said, "He hasn't eaten for a while. And he's tired like everyone else. That makes him grumpy."

"Why hasn't he eaten?" Patrick asked. He formed a cup with his hands. He scooped up some water. Then he tossed it over the edge of the small boat.

The boys peeked between the canvas and the lifeboat.

Another wave hit. It splashed more water into the boat.

"Everyone's seasick. And the storm has people worried," Marcus said.

Patrick's hands were too cold to toss out more water.

"Where'd you come from?" Marcus asked. "I don't remember seeing you earlier."

"My name's Patrick," he said. "I was with Aris before stumbling into Demetrius."

Marcus laughed. "You shortened his name. I like that," he said. "I'll call him Aris too. He's always telling jokes. Have you met Paul?"

"My cousin and I bumped into him. He saved us from being washed over the ship's railing," Patrick said.

Marcus laughed. "He wants to save everyone," he said. "Paul tells stories about a man who rose from the dead. He says that man died on a cross to pay for our sins. I don't know if that's true."

"It is true! Paul is talking about Jesus," Patrick said. "Jesus is the way to God the Father. People who believe in Jesus are forgiven for their sins. They start a relationship with God."

The ship suddenly plunged down the side of a large wave.

Patrick felt his stomach drop, like he was on a roller coaster.

The ship righted itself and started up another wave.

Marcus said, "I was raised by my grandmother. We lived on a small island called Malta. She never needed gods. I don't either."

Suddenly a harsh voice ordered, "Get out of there!"

"Oh no," Marcus said. "We've been found."

Patrick shivered. He would be glad to get out of the cold water. Sooner or later, he would have to face Demetrius. Now was as good a time as any.

"This boat is not a toy," the voice yelled.

A large hand grabbed Patrick by the back of his tunic. Another hand yanked Marcus out of the boat.

"Ow!" Marcus said.

Patrick looked up. The man holding them wasn't Demetrius. He was a sailor.

What have we done? Patrick wondered.

The Tackle

It's hard to tell day from night. The sky is always dark, Beth thought.

Life on the ship was the same. The people sat on the deck in the storm. There wasn't much to do.

Beth remembered the excitement from two days ago. Patrick told her all about it. Patrick met a new friend named Marcus.

They had a run-in with a grouchy soldier.

Then an angry sailor tossed them out of their hiding place. Paul showed up just in time to calm everyone down.

Getting to know Marcus helped to fill the time.

Then there was the aloe oil.

Luke didn't use the aloe oil on Beth's injured arm again. "Your scrape is healing well," he had told her. He had even removed her bandage.

For two days Beth tried to get the oil from Luke's pouch. She wanted to show it to Patrick. But Luke kept the pouch close.

Beth's stomach growled. But she couldn't eat. Luke called it seasickness.

Everyone was seasick. No one had eaten anything for the last two days.

"Ginger soothes the stomach," Luke said. "But my supply has run out."

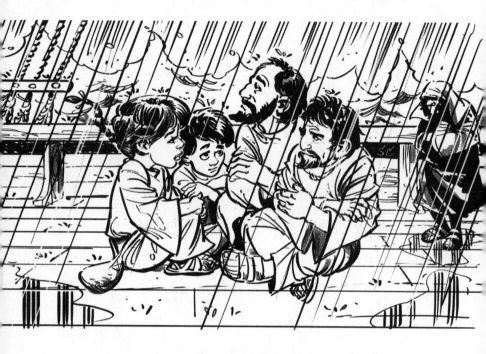

"I like peppermint better than ginger," Aris said.

"Peppermint soothes stomachs?" Beth asked. She reached into her pouch. "Maybe these leaves will help."

Aris held up a rope with a knot in it. He said, "Maybe, or maybe knot." He laughed.

A sailor near him laughed too.

Luke smiled. He said, "You're full of

surprises, Beth. I will crush these into powder. They should help you and others." He left.

Patrick stretched and sat up. "Did you get the aloe oil?" he whispered.

Beth shook her head no. "I'm going to ask Luke for it today," Beth said. "No more sneaking around."

"It's worth a try," Patrick said. The sailor who had found Patrick in the boat walked by. He scowled and shook his head at Patrick.

Patrick turned toward Paul. "Thanks again for saving me from that huge sailor," he said. "I don't know why he's so angry."

"Tempers explode when people are tired and scared," Paul said.

Paul stretched. He said, "Where's your friend Marcus?"

Patrick said, "He's working again."

Beth knew Marcus and Patrick liked hanging out together.

"Let's play 'spot Marcus,'" she said.

"You're on," Patrick said.

Beth scanned the deck. Marcus wasn't bailing water with the other sailors.

Beth looked toward the coils of rope. He wasn't tying furniture down. She looked at the people near them. He wasn't sleeping either.

"I found him," Patrick said. "He's running toward us."

Marcus looked upset.

"What's wrong?" Paul asked.

"The ship's still too heavy," he said. "Throwing the cargo into the sea days ago wasn't enough."

"Oh crate," Aris said. "Get it?" He laughed.

Beth saw Patrick smile.

Marcus didn't seem to hear him. "Everything has to be tossed," Marcus said.

Beth felt the ship climb another wave. The mast rolled on the deck in front of them.

"Even the tackle?" Paul asked.

"Yes," Marcus said. "The ropes, benches, and the rest of the furniture have to go. You grab the tackle at the bow," Marcus said to Paul. "The other sailors and I will toss things at the stern."

"I'll help you," Patrick said.

"We can always use an extra hand," Marcus said. "Let's go."

Patrick hurried away with Marcus.

Paul wrapped his cloak tighter and looked at Beth. "Ready?" he asked.

"I am," she said.

Aris smiled. "I guess the ocean is trying to greet us," he said.

Beth looked at him questioningly.

"It keeps waving," Aris said. He picked up a mat.

Beth laughed. A bucket slid by her. She picked it up.

Everyone looked tired, even Paul. But

everyone helped. Tiredness didn't stop a single person from throwing the tackle overboard.

Paul grabbed a rope. He rolled it between his bent elbow and his hand.

Luke hurried over to them. He started pushing a bench toward the edge of the ship. "The water makes it easier to slide," he said. His foot slipped. "Both for benches and men."

"I'll help you," Aris said. They worked together.

Another wave sloshed over them.

Beth tossed the bucket. She went back and picked up a tangled net. It felt slimy like snakes.

Paul flung the coiled rope into the sea.

Beth threw the net overboard.

Lightning shot across the sky.

The four of them walked back to the center of the ship.

"Does this go?" Beth asked. She pointed to the broken mast.

Paul nodded.

The four of them lined up beside the heavy pole.

"One, two, three, push," Paul said. "One, two, three, push."

Others joined them.

Each push brought the pole closer to the edge of the ship.

The ship dipped.

"Look out!" Beth said.

A giant wave rose in the air. It was double the size of the ship.

Beth's stomach lurched. She held her breath.

The wave shoved Beth backward. It pushed the mast and a bundle of rope backward too.

Beth held her breath. She grabbed the thick pole and hugged it tight. She was sliding way too fast.

A loud shriek filled the air.

Beth had felt like screaming. But the shriek hadn't come from her.

6

Aloe Oil

Beth turned toward the shriek. She saw Aris
hugging the pole near her. His face was
scrunched up. They slid all the way across
the ship toward the opposite railing.

Beth looked around. Paul was helping stop
other people from sliding.

Beth felt the railing smash into her back.
She moaned in pain. The bundle of rope was
between the pole and the rail. The rope had

stopped the pole from squishing her. But she couldn't get out from between the pole and the ship's railing. She was trapped.

Aris said, "Ugh!" He was pinned also. He gasped for air. But it didn't sound like he was getting any.

"Paul!" Beth yelled.

Aris didn't say anything else. His face was losing its color.

"Help!" Beth cried.

Paul ran toward them.

Luke did too.

"Quick," Paul yelled. "Pull the mast away. We need to free Beth and Aris."

Paul, Luke, and others tugged at the pole. Beth pushed.

The pole slid a few inches.

Beth slid out. She saw something caught in the rope coil. It was long and made of cloth. It was Luke's medicine pouch.

"Your pouch," Beth shouted. She pointed to it.

Luke nodded. But he kept holding the pole with the other men.

Beth stepped toward the pouch. She wanted to save the aloe oil. But Aris's face was contorted in pain. Beth hurried to him instead. She grabbed his arms and pulled.

Aris used his legs to push.

The ship rocked.

Luke grunted.

Aris was finally free from the mast. He gasped for air.

Paul let go of the pole. "Don't try to stand, Aris," Paul said. "Luke?"

Luke let go of the pole. He grabbed his medicine pouch from the rope. Then he knelt down beside Aris. Luke took a vial out of his bag.

Aris's eyes were closed.

Beth gathered with others around him.

Luke put the small vial under Aris's nose. The salts in the vial smelled like a strong cleaning liquid.

Aris's eyes opened quickly. He gasped.

"You had the air knocked out of you," Luke said. "How do you feel?"

"Like I fought a pole and lost," Aris said.

The ship tilted. The mast slammed back into the side.

That would have killed us, Beth thought.

"Let's throw that mast overboard," Paul said. The men and Beth lined up next to the pole.

"This mast won't hurt anyone ever again," Beth said.

Paul said, "Ready? Heave!"

Beth picked up the pole with everyone else. The group lifted it above the railing.

The bundle of rope caught on the pole. It flew in the wind. Then it dropped into the waves. The pole went with it and snapped in two like a toothpick.

I'm glad we don't have to jump into the sea, Beth thought. She turned around. The deck was clear. There was nothing left to throw overboard.

Aris looked better. Every breath brought color back into his face.

Paul helped him up. They walked with everyone toward the center of the ship.

Nothing protected them from the rain, wind, and waves now. All they had was each other.

Beth took a deep breath and turned to Luke. "Could I show Patrick the aloe oil?" she asked. "He'd really like to see it."

"Of course," Luke said. He opened his pouch and looked inside. Then he shook his head. "Some of my vials are missing. They must have fallen out. The aloe oil is gone."

"No!" Beth said. *Why didn't I ask Luke to see it earlier?* she thought.

Patrick thought about the aloe oil. It had been days since Beth had told him it was lost. But he still wondered if aloe oil was the liquid the Imagination Station needed.

Luke sat down on the deck next to him.

"Where does aloe come from?" Patrick asked.

Luke turned to him. "That's an odd question," he said.

Patrick shrugged and said, "There's nothing to do but think."

Luke nodded. "Aloe comes from a plant," he said with a yawn. "It grows in many places around this sea." He lay down next to Marcus. Luke shut his eyes and began to snore.

Patrick sighed. Nothing had changed for days. There was no sun to show when it was daytime. There were no stars to show when it was nighttime. The sky was black with clouds and rain. The ship had been in this storm now for fourteen days.

Will it ever end? he wondered.

"What will we do today?" Aris asked. "Is anyone up for a swim?"

Beth smiled.

"Be quiet," a voice in the darkness said. "Quit your jokes. There's no hope. We are all lost."

"All we have left to do is die," another said.

"What are you talking about?" Paul asked. His lips were curved in a smile. "God gives us every breath as a gift. You don't know what the day will bring. That is reason enough for hope."

Patrick sighed. His stomach rumbled. Luke had given him peppermint days ago. It had settled his stomach. But now even it was gone.

The bread Patrick had tried to eat earlier had not stayed down. He closed his eyes again.

Paul stood. Wind whipped the edge of his cloak. Rain poured down his face.

People turned toward him.

"Men, you should have listened to me," Paul said. "We shouldn't have left Crete."

Patrick sighed. "It's too late for that now," he said.

"It's not too late," Paul said. "I have heard from God."

The Fourteenth Day

Another wave splashed over Patrick. Beth looked as cold, tired, wet, and hungry as he felt.

"Take heart," Paul said. "No one among us will die."

"You can't know that," Demetrius said.

"But I do. This very night an angel stood before me," Paul said. He paused. Some of the people around Patrick sat up to listen more closely.

Paul said, "The angel came from my God. He said, 'Do not be afraid, Paul. You must stand before Caesar.'"

Demetrius stood. "That sounds good for you," he said. "Not us."

"Maybe there's more," Beth said.

Patrick hoped there was. He knew Paul had slept. Paul was one of the few who had. Maybe God spoke to Paul through a dream.

Paul smiled. He said, "The angel said God would spare everyone on this ship."

"Really?" Beth asked.

"Things will happen exactly as I have told you," Paul said.

"That's nonsense," Demetrius said. He put on his helmet.

"Nothing's changed yet," Aris said. "But it

will. You'll see. Then perhaps you'll believe in our God too."

Demetrius said, "I doubt we'll get out of this alive. If we do, I'll listen to your babbling. But not a moment before." He stomped away.

"Maybe the storm will suddenly stop," Patrick said.

"Maybe another ship will rescue us," Aris said.

Luke's snoring grew louder.

"Maybe large birds will carry us to land," Patrick said.

"Oooh," Aris said. "I like that one. I think I'll dream about that. Good night." Aris stretched out next to Luke.

"Sleep well, Aris," Paul said. "Soon you'll get the chance to tell Demetrius about Jesus." He stretched out also.

Patrick walked over to the railing. He

listened to the *pit-pat* of raindrops and the rumble of thunder.

Beth joined him.

There was a great burst of wind. Patrick heard the crashing of waves.

Beth said, "I hear something."

Then Patrick heard it too. It sounded like water was slapping something hard, like a sidewalk. He and Beth hurried back to their friends.

Marcus moaned in his sleep.

Patrick shook him.

"What?" Marcus asked.

"Listen," Beth said.

Marcus sat up and tilted his head to listen. Marcus's eyebrows went up.

"The waves are hitting something," Patrick said. "What are they hitting?"

"Rocks!" Marcus said. "We have to tell the centurion!" He jumped up.

Patrick and Beth stood too. They followed Marcus through the sleeping men and ran toward the stern.

Patrick saw a man in a short tunic in the distance. He wore a metal breastplate and metal skirt over his tunic. The man's helmet sported a bright-red plume.

"Will that man know what to do?" Beth asked.

"Yes, Julius is a centurion. When he enters a battle, he leads the troops. When he steps onto a Roman ship," Marcus said, "he becomes the person in charge. The ship's captain will obey him."

Julius was talking to soldiers.

Demetrius took a double look at Patrick,

Beth, and Marcus. He stepped in their way. "Stop!" he said. He had an angry glint in his eyes.

"We must speak to the centurion," Patrick said.

"It's urgent," Beth said.

Demetrius's eyes narrowed. He didn't move.

"*Ave*, my centurion," Marcus yelled. He beat his fist to his chest.

"What does 'ah-vey' mean?" Patrick whispered.

Beth shrugged.

"Ave, my centurion," Marcus shouted louder.

Patrick trusted Marcus. He started yelling, "Ave, my centurion!"

Beth yelled it too.

"Quiet!" Demetrius said. "What good is 'ave' now? You can't tell him to be well. No one can be well in this storm!"

"Rocks!" yelled Marcus. "We're nearing rocks!"

Julius raised his hand. The children stopped yelling. Everyone stopped talking.

The centurion listened. "I hear it," he said.

Patrick breathed a sigh of relief.

Julius said, "Bring those children here."

Marcus walked forward quickly.

Demetrius grabbed the scruff of Patrick's neck. He moved Beth forward with his other hand. He didn't let go until they were in front of Julius. Just as quickly, Demetrius released them and left.

"Take a sounding," Julius said.

"Yes, my centurion," Marcus said. He turned to Patrick and Beth. "Follow me."

The children hurried to the far end of the stern.

"What are we doing?" Patrick asked.

"Measuring the sea," Marcus said. He took

a long, thin piece of metal from a chest. It had a rounded cap at the bottom. A long, knotted leather rope was attached to it.

"That looks like a bell. How does it work?" Beth asked.

"It isn't a bell," Marcus said. "It's a weight."

Marcus dropped the weight into the water. He held on to the rope.

The rope had knots every six feet or so. Marcus slowly fed the rope into the sea.

"You're counting the knots," Patrick said.

Marcus nodded.

Patrick peered into the stormy night. *We must be close to land if we hear waves hitting rocks,* he thought.

"The weight has reached the bottom," Marcus said. "The water is one hundred twenty feet deep. Tell the centurion." He started rolling up the knotted rope.

Patrick ran as fast as he could on the slippery deck. The ends of his belt flew sideways in the wind. Finally, he reached Julius. Patrick stumbled forward.

"Ave, my centurion," Patrick said. "The sea is one hundred twenty feet deep."

Julius gave a single nod. "Again," he said.

Patrick turned. He slid only once on his way back to Beth and Marcus.

The knotted rope was in Beth's hands.

"We have to measure again," Patrick said.

Marcus nodded. "Throw the weight into the sea, Beth," he said. "It will continue to go down until it reaches the sea floor."

Beth threw the weight into the sea. She counted the knots as they went into the water after it.

"Why does he want it measured again?" Patrick asked.

"A smaller number means we are headed toward land," Marcus said. "A larger measure means we're headed away from land."

Beth said, "We are at ninety feet."

Marcus frowned.

Patrick knew why. The ship might be headed toward a rocky shore. The ship could be dashed to pieces.

Four Anchors

Beth was out of breath by the time they reached the centurion.

Marcus said, "We're at ninety feet."

Julius's eyebrows rose. "Drop the anchors," he commanded.

Sailors rushed across the deck. Marcus hurried to help them.

Beth and Patrick moved to the side and watched.

"This might be a good thing," Beth said.

Patrick gave her an odd look. He said, "Crashing into rocks?"

"No," she said. "Didn't Luke say aloe grows in many places around this sea?" She smiled.

"I understand," Patrick said. "We can find an aloe plant once we're on land. We can test it with Whit's gadget."

Beth watched the sailors work. The anchors were bigger than the sailors.

One by one all four anchors were lowered into the sea.

The ship slowed.

"How will we get to shore?" Patrick asked. "We can't swim. The waves are too wild."

Beth knew that was true. She'd seen the mast snapped in two by the waves.

The ship came to a stop. The lines to the

anchors were tight. The anchors kept the ship from moving forward.

"I have an idea," Patrick said. "There's a lifeboat on deck. Maybe we can row it to land and find the aloe ourselves. We could be back at Whit's End before breakfast."

"I didn't know they had lifeboats on Roman ships," Beth said. "Do they have enough for everyone?"

"I don't know," Patrick said. "But I'll show you the one I saw." He started walking away from the back of the ship.

Beth walked with him. Her tunic slapped her legs. It felt good to be doing something. She was tired of being on the ship.

The cousins reached the bow.

Patrick pointed. "The lifeboat used to be right there," he said.

Beth looked where he was pointing. A group of sailors was looking over the side of the ship.

"Maybe someone moved it," Beth said. She walked to the railing and looked over. She saw one wooden lifeboat partway down to the sea.

Sailors were lowering the boat.

"Excuse me," Beth said. "Where are the other lifeboats?"

The ship rocked to one side. Thunder boomed and rain poured down.

Beth grabbed the railing to keep from falling.

The sailors scowled at her.

"We're throwing smaller anchors into the sea," a sailor said.

Patrick looked at Beth and then at the sailors. "No, you aren't. You're lowering the small boat," he said.

One of the sailors came toward them. "You don't understand," he said. He seemed nervous. "To release the smaller anchors, we go out in the lifeboat. We don't drop them next to the ship."

"But you don't have any anchors," Patrick said.

"You children get out of here," another sailor said. "We have work to do."

Beth turned to Patrick. "Let's find a different lifeboat," she said.

"I didn't see any others on our way here," Patrick said.

"Is there only one?" Beth asked

"Maybe." Patrick held on to the railing. He said, "I wonder what the sailors are really doing with the boat."

"I don't know," Beth said. "I feel bad. We were thinking of taking the only lifeboat."

"I feel bad too," Patrick said. "I don't think our plan would have worked anyway. The boat looked too heavy for us. Let's find Paul. He'll know what the sailors were doing."

The cousins walked back to the center of the ship.

Paul, Aris, and Luke were on their knees in prayer. "Mighty Lord," Paul said, "I know you have promised to keep us safe. Now I pray for daylight."

Lightning flashed. It lit up the deck.

Beth was surprised. Those three men weren't the only ones praying. People all over the deck were praying. Some were praying with loud cries and groans.

Are they afraid the ship is going to hit the rocks? she wondered.

A Final Meal

Paul finished praying. He smiled. "Ah, you have just missed being refreshed through prayer," he said.

But not all the passengers looked refreshed.

Patrick frowned. He had missed praying with Paul.

"And we've come looking for you. Something strange is happening," Beth said.

"What is that?" Paul asked. He leaned in closer.

"Before I explain that, Patrick and I have something to confess," Beth said. "We wanted to find an aloe plant."

"On the ship?" Luke asked. He chuckled softly.

"No," Patrick said. "We were going to take one of the lifeboats. We thought we could row to land. The ship is close to the shore. We didn't know there was only one lifeboat."

"But sailors were already using it," Beth said. "They might be leaving the ship."

"What?" Paul said. His voice carried across the deck.

Luke leaned toward them. "Are you sure?" he asked.

"They said they were lowering anchors," Beth said.

"They would need the lifeboat to drop small

anchors," Aris said. "Very dangerous but quite common."

Patrick said, "But there weren't any anchors in the lifeboat."

Aris frowned.

"Julius needs to know," Paul said. He stood and started walking. "Come. You must tell him what you saw and heard," he said.

The wind caused Paul's cloak to billow around him.

The cousins followed him. Luke and Aris did too.

Once again, Patrick and Beth found themselves in front of Julius.

Paul told him, "I had a dream. The Lord told me I would stand trial before Caesar. He said the lives of everyone on this ship would be saved."

Julius frowned. He said, "I'm not interested in listening to dreams, Paul."

Paul said, "You should have listened to me earlier. We should have stayed the winter at Fair Havens. Don't make the same mistake now. Whether we live or die is your decision."

Julius looked into the storm.

"Patrick," Paul said, "tell the centurion what you saw."

Patrick took a step forward. "Sailors have lowered a small boat into the sea," he said.

Then Paul said in a loud voice, "These men must stay with the ship, or *you* won't be saved."

Julius looked at Paul. "Demetrius, take a group of men," he said. "Cut the ropes to the lifeboat."

Demetrius pointed to a couple of soldiers. They left with him.

Beth knew the soldiers would obey Julius's orders.

"Now," Paul said. "It's time to eat. No one has eaten in a long time."

Julius seemed annoyed. "Everyone is seasick," he said.

Paul said, "They need their strength. My God has told me that not one person will die. But the ship will be harmed."

Patrick's eyes grew large. *Would the ship be wrecked?* he wondered.

Julius said, "You children, do what he says. Have the people eat. Then we'll lighten the ship." He nodded for soldiers to go with them too.

"How can we lighten the ship?" Beth asked Patrick. "Everything has been thrown overboard."

"You're right," Patrick said. He thought for a moment. Paul had told them this was a grain ship. He said, "He's going to dump the grain."

"Oh," Beth said.

Paul headed back toward the center of the ship.

Patrick and Beth followed.

The rest of the passengers were starting to wake up.

Patrick thought it had to be near dawn. The night had to be almost over.

Soldiers brought bread to Paul. Then sailors, merchants, passengers, and soldiers gathered around him.

In a loud voice, Paul prayed, "Thank you, God, for this food."

Paul tore off a piece of bread. He began to eat it.

Others came forward and took bread from the soldiers. They started eating too.

Patrick took a piece. The rain made it soggy.

Beth ate also. "It feels like something is about to happen," she said.

"I have the same feeling," Patrick said. He took a bite. "Paul said we'd need our strength."

Patrick took another bite of wet bread. Whatever was going to happen was going to happen soon.

Narrow Passage

Marcus joined Beth and Patrick. "It's a good thing I like soggy bread," he said.

Aris held two loaves in his hands. "Which one should I choose?" he asked. "It's such a tough dough-cision."

Marcus laughed.

Others smiled.

Beth swallowed a chunk of bread. It stopped her stomach from growling.

Julius walked up to the group. "Bread, please," he said.

A soldier gave him a loaf.

Julius started to eat it.

"We're eating with a centurion," someone said.

Several people laughed.

The meal felt like a large picnic. Beth saw a mighty wave rise above the ship.

"Even the waves cannot dampen our mood," Aris said. "Only our bread."

Beth shook her head. But she smiled.

Aris laughed.

Julius smiled. That made others smile.

Julius finished eating. The mood immediately turned serious.

Beth felt the change. She swallowed a final soggy chunk of bread.

"Release the grain," Julius said. "The ship must be lightened. The anchors can only hold us for so long."

Sailors and soldiers left together to carry out Julius's order.

"Look behind us," Patrick said. "Dawn has finally come."

Beth turned. She saw the glimmer of light on the horizon. Perhaps the storm was almost over. She turned back. Were her eyes playing tricks on her?

"Is that a beach?" she asked. She blinked. It was still there.

"That's land!" Patrick said.

The people around them raised a cheer.

Marcus gasped. "I know this place.
I recognize it," he said. "My grandmother
lives here."

Julius walked over to Marcus. "Tell me all
you know," he said.

Marcus stepped forward. "This bay leads to
a sandy beach," he said. "And there is a village
not far from here."

Beth turned to Patrick. "We're saved!" she
said.

"Perhaps," Julius said. "This harbor is our
last hope. The ship won't survive another day.
It may not last another hour."

"It won't be easy to get to shore," Marcus
said. "There is a sandbar reef beneath the
surface. There is only a narrow passage
through it."

"Hoist the foresail to the wind," Julius
yelled. "Untie the rudders."

Beth nibbled her bottom lip. *Could this*

large ship make it through a narrow passage? she wondered.

"Our chances don't look good," Patrick said.

"Our hope is not in what we see," Paul said. "Our hope is in God alone. It always has been."

Julius stood at the bow. "Brace yourselves," he said. His voice carried across the deck of the ship.

"Cut loose the anchors," Julius said. "We are going through." He paused. Then he said, "May Paul's God guide us."

The ship burst forward. It sped directly toward the beach.

Patrick saw the land grow closer.

We could be there in minutes, he thought.

Crashing water from one direction slammed into the back of the ship. The front of the ship jerked to the side. It hit the reef.

Patrick was thrown onto the slippery deck. "Ow!" he said.

Beth fell beside him. So did everyone else.

But Patrick jumped up quickly. He looked toward the shore.

Beth stood.

It's only three soccer fields away, he thought.

Marcus yelled, "The front of the ship has hit a sandbar."

The ship didn't move.

"We're stuck," Julius said.

The wind and waves smashed against the back of the ship.

Crack!

A large section of the stern broke off.

"We're going to sink," Patrick said.

The ship's deck tilted.

"I thought your God was going to save us, Paul!" a voice said.

"God said our lives would be saved," Luke said. "He didn't say the ship would survive."

Waves pelted them. Wood from the ship flew into the sea.

Paul moved toward Julius.

Cold greenish-gray water swirled around the ship. Rain poured from the heavens.

"The sea is going to tear the ship to bits," Beth said.

Thunder rumbled.

The Roman soldiers moved closer together. They started whispering.

Patrick heard Demetrius say, "Wait for the next wave. Then draw your swords."

Patrick looked at them. *How would that stop the ship from falling apart?* he wondered.

"Why should we draw our swords?" a young soldier asked.

"To kill the prisoners," Demetrius said.

"You can't!" Patrick yelled.

The soldiers glared at him.

Demetrius growled.

Patrick's heart beat faster. "Beth, they're going to kill the prisoners," he said.

"No!" Beth exclaimed. "We've got to get to Paul," Beth said. "Or Luke, or Aris. We have to tell them what's going on."

A wave began to form. It rose high above them.

Patrick saw Paul by Julius with a group of prisoners.

Patrick said, "We have to tell Julius!"

The wave fell on them.

Demetrius and the other soldiers drew their swords.

Lightning flashed. It reflected on the steel blades.

"Julius!" Patrick screamed. "Save Paul!"

"Protect Aris!" Beth yelled.

The soldiers charged.

Prisoners around Paul shrieked.

"Halt!" Julius yelled. He drew his sword.

The prisoners hid behind him.

Paul and Aris stepped forward.

Demetrius stopped. The other soldiers stopped too.

"You will not harm Paul," Julius's voice thundered. "Or any of the prisoners."

Demetrius kept his sword raised. "Rome will kill us if a single prisoner escapes," Demetrius said. "It's us or them."

A Long Swim

Julius glared at Demetrius. He held his sword steady.

"Paul is a man of God," Julius said. "Do you want his God to be against us?"

"Where has his God gotten us?" Demetrius said. "We are shipwrecked. Many will die."

"No one will die," Paul said. "Only the ship will be destroyed."

"Will you go against Caesar's law?" Demetrius asked. "Do you want *him* against us?"

Julius paused. Then he said, "I'll take personal responsibility for the prisoners."

Demetrius glared. The rest of the soldiers behind him sheathed their swords. Finally, Demetrius did too.

Beth looked at the prisoners. They looked relieved.

The grain ship trembled on the waves.

"Watch out!" Beth said. She pointed to a piece of wood flying toward them.

Patrick and Beth dropped onto the slimy deck.

Luke and Aris fell flat beside them. So did Paul and Julius.

The board flew over them. But it hit two soldiers. They grunted in surprise. But they weren't hurt. Their armor kept them from harm.

Beth hopped up. "The ship is being torn apart," she said.

Patrick, Aris, and Luke stood up.

Aris said, "I've never seen a plank fly before. Butterfly, sure. But not wood."

Julius raised his hand.

Everyone was quiet.

"Swimmers," Julius said, "jump into the sea and get to land."

Immediately passengers and prisoners flung themselves into the waves.

Beth knew how to swim. So did Patrick. But Beth remembered how the sea broke the large mast in half. What would it do to them?

Paul walked to the edge of the ship. "It's time to go ashore," he said. Then he climbed the railing and jumped into the water.

Aris went next. He jumped off the ship and pretended to run in the air.

Luke laughed. He tied his medical pouch

tightly to his body. Then he dove into the waves too.

Beth looked over the edge of the ship.

Each of their heads bobbed above the surface. The men started swimming to shore.

Marcus came from behind them. "You two are next," he said. "I'll follow."

Beth gave Patrick and Marcus a brave smile. She climbed the railing and jumped into the sea.

"Keep your eyes on the beach," Marcus yelled.

The water was freezing. The salt stung her eyes. Beth began to do the crawl stroke. Her face was in the sea and then out for a breath. She forced her feet to kick.

The crawl stroke worked in swimming pools. But here she didn't have the same power. The waves were too strong.

What am I going to do? she wondered.

Patrick reached into his pouch. He took out his swimming goggles. They would keep the saltwater out of his eyes. He looked for Beth in the water.

"There she is," Marcus said. "May your and Paul's God guide you both."

Patrick leaned against the ship's railing. "And may He guide you," Patrick said.

Crack!

The railing gave way.

Patrick fell. He had time for one deep breath. Then he plunged into the sea.

The icy water stung. The saltwater poured over his lips and into his mouth.

Patrick pushed back to the surface and spit it out. He put on his goggles. Then he tilted them to dump the saltwater out of them.

Patrick tried to swim ashore. But his foot

was caught. Patrick took a breath and ducked underwater. Tall seagrass had wrapped around one of his sandals. His goggles helped him to see it.

He pulled the seagrass away from his sandals. Then Patrick pushed back to the surface. He gulped in air. But he was turned around. He was facing the ship.

Marcus jumped into the water. He landed close to Patrick.

A wave crashed into them.

A plank swooshed by them.

Patrick dodged it.

Marcus rose to the surface.

"Something's grabbing my feet," Marcus cried. He took a deep breath and went down.

Patrick ducked underwater too.

Marcus's feet were tangled in seagrass. The more he kicked, the more trapped he became.

Patrick tore at the seagrass. He almost had Marcus free.

But Marcus started to sink. He was drowning!

Patrick freed his friend from the seagrass. He pulled Marcus to the surface.

Another plank floated by.

Patrick grabbed it. He draped Marcus over it. Then he held on to the plank and kicked toward the shore.

Waves kept crashing into Beth. She saw Patrick and Marcus behind her.

What is Patrick doing? she wondered. He was holding on to something. It was a plank from the ship.

That's what she needed. There were pieces of the ship all around her. She had been dodging them.

Beth saw a plank the right size. She swam toward it. Her arms pounded the water. Her legs kicked with force.

Another wave came. She dove toward the plank. She grabbed it and leaned on it like a paddle board. She began to kick.

Julius's voice came from behind her. "Abandon ship," he yelled. "Grab a plank. Use it to help you get to shore."

Beth looked at the beach. Someone had started a bonfire. She kept her eyes on the flames.

Kick. Kick. Kick.

Finally, one of her knees hit sand. She could touch the bottom. Beth let go of the plank

and walked to shore. Then she fell onto the wet beach.

Thank you, God, she thought. She lay there for a moment to catch her breath. Finally, she sat up. *Where's Patrick?* she wondered.

People from the ship were dragging themselves through the shallow water. Some were already lying on the beach.

"Patrick," Beth yelled. She scanned the waves.

"Come to the fire," a woman's voice called.

People walked toward the warmth. Villagers passed out food and drink. They put blankets around shivering people.

Beth saw Luke walk toward the fire. She saw Demetrius move toward it also.

"Patrick," Beth yelled again. Her voice sounded small.

Then she saw him. He was farther down the beach.

Beth forced herself to stand up. Her legs felt shaky. But she started running toward Patrick. She had to be sure he was all right.

Patrick stumbled out of the water. He was dragging someone with him.

Deadly Bite

Patrick pulled Marcus out of the water and onto the beach. He threw off his goggles. Then he dropped onto the sand.

Beth reached Patrick and dropped onto the sand next to him.

Julius came out of the water behind them. He knelt by Marcus.

"He's swallowed too much seawater," Julius

said. Then he turned Marcus on his side and slapped his back. "Go find Paul's doctor."

"He's by the fire," Beth said.

Patrick ran toward the fire. "Luke," he yelled.

Luke was on the outside of the crowd. He stood next to Paul and Aris. Luke and Paul turned toward Patrick.

"Marcus needs help," he said. Patrick pointed in Marcus's direction.

Luke and Paul looked cold and tired. But they hurried toward Marcus.

Luke untied his pouch as he ran.

Aris didn't move. He reached out an arm to Patrick.

"I need help," he said. "My spirit is willing, but my body is weak."

Patrick put Aris's arm over his shoulders. But he didn't take him to Marcus. Instead, Patrick saw Demetrius warming himself.

Patrick brought Aris closer to the fire. He helped Aris sit down next to Demetrius.

"Get warm," Patrick said.

Aris gave Patrick a grateful smile. He extended his hands toward the flames and looked at Demetrius.

"Are you ready to hear about Jesus?" Aris asked softly.

Demetrius cleared his voice. "I'm a man of my word. I shall listen," he said.

Patrick smiled. He ran back to Marcus. He passed Julius on the way.

Julius was heading toward the fire.

"Is Marcus okay?" Patrick asked.

"He's breathing," Julius said.

Patrick gave a sigh of relief. He kept running. Soon he was by Marcus's side.

Luke was putting a vial back into his pouch. He turned to Patrick.

"Can you help me take Marcus to the fire?" he asked.

"Of course," Patrick said. He turned to Marcus. "We can ask the islanders about your grandmother."

Julius's voice boomed across the beach. "I need volunteers to gather more brushwood," he said.

"I'll go," Paul called.

"Me too," Beth said.

Patrick put Marcus's arm over his shoulders.

"There used to be more brushwood that way," Marcus said softly. He pointed down the beach. "Be careful of vipers."

"He means snakes with venom," Luke said. He put Marcus's other arm around his shoulders. "Venom is like poison. But it's pushed into the body by the snake's fangs."

"There is no cure for their bite," Marcus said. "Be careful. They look like sticks."

Patrick and Luke started walking toward the fire with Marcus.

Patrick watched the ground. He didn't want to step on a viper.

Beth hurried down the beach away from the fire. She caught up to Paul.

"Can I help you gather brushwood?" she asked him.

Paul smiled. "That would be nice," he said. "We can protect each other from vipers."

Beth looked around. "Brushwood is small branches from trees and bushes, right?" she asked. She had camped last summer in the woods near her home. She thought they had used brushwood to build a fire then.

"You are right," Paul said. "Here, let's go this way."

The two went into a thicket that was off the beach.

"Have you ever seen a viper?" Beth asked. She didn't know how to tell a stick from a viper.

She kicked a branch on the ground.

The stick didn't move.

Beth picked it up.

"Not the vipers on this island," Paul said.

Beth kicked another stick. Then she bent down to pick it up.

"Wait!" Paul cried.

The stick moved. It quickly slid away.

Beth gasped. "That was a viper," she said.

"It's hard to spot them," Paul said. "Jesus once called the teachers of the law and

Pharisees vipers." He smiled. "Their words were as dangerous as a viper's venom. They stopped people from coming to God."

Beth continued kicking each stick. But then she waited a moment. Only then did she pick it up.

Paul asked, "Does anything keep you from God?"

"Sometimes I forget about God," Beth said. "I only think about me and what I want. But then I ask Jesus to forgive me. I know He does." She smiled at Paul.

"You're a believer!" Paul said. He beamed at her.

"I am," she said. "So is Patrick."

"That's very good," Paul said. He picked up another stick. His arms were nearly full. "The most important thing in life is to know Jesus. Nothing matters as much as that."

"I know that's true. But finding aloe also matters to me," Beth said.

"There's quite a bit of aloe here," he said. "This island seems to have aloe everywhere." He laughed.

Paul reached down and picked a plant. "Here you go," he said. He handed it to her.

Beth smiled and said, "Thank you." She put it in her empty pouch.

The two continued to pick up sticks.

"We have as much brushwood as we can carry," Paul said.

Beth nodded.

The two started back toward the beach.

Beth couldn't wait to show Patrick the aloe plant.

The crowd on the beach had grown.

"Brushwood coming through," Paul said.

Beth saw Julius by the fire.

"Let them pass," Julius said.

Red, yellow, and orange flames leaped into the air. They rose as high as Paul was tall.

Paul and Beth moved next to Julius.

"Would you like me to throw your bundle in with mine?" Paul asked.

"Yes," Beth said. She handed her bundle to Paul.

Paul started to toss the brushwood into the flames.

A stick was wiggling out of the pile. "Viper!" Beth yelled.

Paul quickly tossed the sticks.

The snake slithered away from the heat. Its fangs caught Paul's hand. The viper dangled in the air.

People around the fire gasped. They backed away from Paul.

"That viper is deadly," a teen yelled.

Paul shook his hand. The viper fell into the fire.

"You know he's a prisoner," a man's voice whispered.

"He must be a murderer," another said. "The viper bite is the judgment of the gods."

Oh no! Beth thought. *Paul can't die now!*

The Courtyard

Patrick felt the rain stop. He was grateful and leaned toward the fire. The storm was ending, and Marcus was going to be fine. The islanders had helped him find his grandmother. She'd taken him back to her home.

The crowd started backing away from the fire. It was warmer without the rain. But it wasn't that warm.

Patrick looked around. He noticed Beth and Paul on the other side of the bonfire.

117

A villager pointed to Paul. She said, "That man was bitten by a viper."

"Oh no!" Patrick said. He hurried toward Paul and Beth. "What can I do to help?"

Paul smiled. "God said I would stand trial before Caesar," he said. "I won't die here today."

"I'll find Luke," Patrick said. "He'll know what to do."

"No one can help him now," an islander said. "He'll swell up, and then he'll fall down dead. It's a pain-filled death."

"Go get Luke if you must," Paul said. He smiled as if amused.

Patrick ran through the crowd. "Luke," he yelled. "Luke!"

"Over here," Luke said. He was tying a cloth around someone's leg.

Patrick said, "Paul's been bitten by a viper. Come quickly!"

"No one can cure a viper bite," a nearby person said. He waved Luke on. "Go say goodbye to your friend."

Luke stuffed his supplies into his pouch and stood. "Where is he?" he asked.

"This way," Patrick said. He took off running. Luke followed.

They quickly reached Paul.

Everyone but Beth and Julius had moved away from Paul.

"Bring water!" Julius said. "Perhaps water will dilute the venom."

But no one moved. The crowd looked on sadly as if Paul were already dead.

"The villagers say he only has minutes to live," Julius said. Sadness clouded his features.

Paul said, "I won't die today. The puncture wound hurts. But other than that, I'm well."

Luke said, "I can help with the pain. Let me see."

Paul let Luke take a look at his hand.

Patrick studied Paul. He looked weary and worn. But so did everyone else from the ship. Patrick believed Paul. He wouldn't die today.

Luke poured honey on Paul's wound.

Patrick wondered if honey would keep germs away. The crowd kept watching. But nothing happened.

Patrick heard a voice behind the crowd ask, "Where is your leader?"

The crowd opened.

A man dressed like a Roman messenger hurried forward.

"He's over here," Patrick said. He pointed to Julius. The centurion was still standing next to Paul and Luke.

"I am he," Julius said. His voice was loud and commanding.

The messenger said, "The governor of the island invites you to his home. Everyone from the shipwreck may stay the night in his courtyard."

Patrick smiled. Everyone would be taken care of now.

"I thank you on behalf of Rome and myself," Julius said. The two men started speaking to each other.

Patrick looked at Beth. Their help was no longer needed.

Beth motioned for him to follow her.

They moved away from the group.

Beth pulled a plant out of her pouch. "It's an aloe plant," she said. "Maybe it's time for us to go home."

"I'm ready," Patrick said. "Where'd you find the plant?"

"Paul found it for me," she said. "See if it will turn Whit's gadget green."

Patrick took the gadget out of his pouch. He touched the wand to the plant.

The light didn't turn green.

"Maybe you need the juice on the inside of it," Beth said. She broke one of its long leaves in half. Goo dripped out of it.

Patrick touched the wand to it. The green light didn't light up. It didn't even flicker.

"The Imagination Station doesn't need the aloe plant," Beth said.

What liquid did it need? Patrick wondered.

The next morning, Beth saw Marcus in the governor's courtyard. He held a small wooden box in his hands.

"I heard Paul was bitten by a viper, but he

didn't die," he said. "I had to see it for myself. People are saying he's a god. I've never met a god before."

"Paul is not a god," Beth said. "But he serves a powerful God. Paul's God is the only true God!"

Patrick hurried over to them. "Hi, Marcus," he said.

"Hi, Patrick," Marcus said. "Paul's God must be very strong."

"He is," Patrick said. "His son, Jesus, died to pay the price for our sins. Then Jesus rose from the dead. Those who believe what He did for them are saved from their sins. They are given eternal life."

"He's our God. He can be your God too," Beth said. "All you have to do is believe on the name of Jesus."

Paul and Luke walked over to them.

Paul said, "Good morning."

Marcus smiled at him. "Good morning," he said.

Aris joined them.

"I heard there's a ship on the other side of the island," Marcus said. "It's wintering there. We might sail on it in the spring. Until then, I'll be staying with my grandmother."

"Good. Will you join us for a meal now?" Aris asked.

"I can't. I have to bring the oil in this box to the governor," Marcus said. "It's important. My grandmother sent it to him."

"Come back when you're done," Luke said. "I smell food cooking."

"The women from the village are making flat cakes for you," Marcus said. He waved and left them.

The smell made Beth's stomach grumble.

Others started to sniff the air. No one was queasy now. They could finally eat and enjoy it.

People from the village started passing out the flat cakes.

"Thank you," Beth said. She bit into one. It tasted like sweet pancakes.

Patrick ate one too. "Mmm!" he said.

Julius entered the courtyard near them. A man walked beside him. The man was almost bald. He wore a white toga that went to his knees.

Julius said, "That's him." He pointed to Paul.

Roman guards hurried to Paul's side. They grabbed him.

What did Paul do? Beth wondered.

Bambinella

The Roman soldiers held Paul's arms.

"What are you doing?" Beth asked.

Luke and Aris stepped closer to Paul.

"Leave him alone," Patrick said. He reached out a hand toward the soldiers.

"Halt!" Julius said.

Everyone stopped.

"Treat Paul well," Julius said. "We need his services."

The Roman soldiers let go of Paul.

The man next to Julius looked upset. His forehead was creased with worry lines.

Beth moved toward Luke and Aris. "Who is that man?" she asked.

"His name is Publius," Luke whispered. "He's the governor. This is his home."

"Publius's father is dying," Julius said to Paul. "Your God can heal him."

Paul looked concerned.

"Thank you for your hospitality," Paul said. "I would be honored to pray for your father. But that doesn't mean he will be healed."

Beth saw a sad look cross Publius's face.

127

"It's up to God," Paul said. "God may save your father. And He may not."

Publius looked thoughtful.

"Of course," Publius said. "I am a governor. People ask me for many things. Some I give. Others I do not. Your God is the one in power now. I will abide by His choice."

"Good," Paul said. "Show me to your father."

Beth and Patrick followed Paul to a small room off the courtyard.

Marcus was there with his box.

"Publius," he said. "I have brought oil from my grandmother to anoint your father."

"Thank you," Publius said. He took the box from Marcus. "But first Paul will pray for him."

Everyone turned toward Paul.

Will there be another miracle? Beth wondered.

Patrick looked at Publius's father. The man lay on a bed with beautiful carvings. His face was pale. He was groaning and writhing.

An older woman sat next to him. Tears fell down her cheeks.

Publius stood in the corner. He held Marcus's box of oil. He looked sad.

Marcus stood near him.

Paul knelt before the bed. He put his hands on the man. He prayed for him silently.

Patrick wasn't sure what to do.

But then Paul stopped praying.

"It is up to your God now," Publius said.

The room grew quiet. They all waited to see what would happen.

Patrick watched Publius's father.

Suddenly the sick man sat up. "Why are you all so sad?" he asked. He smiled.

Patrick couldn't believe it. A sick man was healed!

The woman next to Publius's father laughed.

Publius handed the box back to Marcus. "Thank your grandmother," he said. "But we no longer have any need of your family's special oils." Then Publius hurried to his father and helped him stand up.

"Who is your God?" Publius asked Paul.

"He is the Lord God Almighty, maker of heaven and earth," Paul said. "His Son's name is Jesus." Paul smiled.

Beth smiled too.

"We must know more about your God," Publius said.

"I can tell you all about Him," Paul said with a smile. "I have nowhere to go until spring."

Marcus brought the box of oil to Patrick. "My grandmother makes this from Bambinella pears, apricots, lemons, and oranges. All these fruits grow on this island," he said.

"The seed oil is a family recipe that only she knows. Please take it. I want to thank you for saving me," Marcus said.

"You don't have to thank me," Patrick said.

"I know," Marcus said. "But I want to." Marcus took a vial out of the box. He handed the vial to Patrick.

"Thank you," Patrick said.

"I'd better go now," Marcus said. "I have to tell my grandmother what happened. Then I need to learn more about your powerful God."

Beth waved goodbye to Marcus.

Patrick turned to Beth. "Could this be the liquid we need?" he asked.

They hurried out of the room and into the courtyard.

Patrick took Whit's gadget out of his pouch. He opened the vial. Then he stuck the wand of his gadget into the liquid. The light on the box turned green.

Patrick heard the hum of the Imagination Station.

"There it is," Beth said.

It appeared in front of them.

Beth jumped into the driver's seat.

Patrick hopped into the passenger side.

A small key was in the lock next to an open compartment. Patrick put the vial with the seed oil into it. He turned the key in the lock.

A sliding panel covered the compartment. Then the panel opened. The container full of oil was no longer there. The oil was now inside the Imagination Station.

Patrick left the key in the lock. They had found two of the liquids the Imagination Station needed. Patrick couldn't wait to tell Whit about this adventure.

"Let's see if we can make it home this time," Beth said. She hit the red button in the middle of the steering wheel. Nothing happened.

Then slowly the sunlight dimmed around them.

Has the Imagination Station finally broken? Patrick wondered. It felt like they were stuck in an empty tunnel.

Suddenly the Imagination Station took off at top speed. Lights flashed all around them. A long and slow whistle blew.

The flashing lights began to swirl. Patrick saw an image of Mr. Whittaker tinkering in his workshop.

"We're almost home!" Patrick cried.

The image grew blurry. Colorful dots swirled around them.

"No!" Beth yelled.

Patrick smelled apricots, lemons, oranges, and Bambinella pears.

Then everything went black.

Secret Word Puzzle

God saved all 276 people on a shipwrecked boat. He saved Paul from a viper's poison. And He healed Publius's father.

Cross out all the letters X, B, and J in the puzzle. Follow the gray line. Write the remaining letters on the lines below the puzzle. That will reveal your eight-letter, secret word!

Secret Word Puzzle

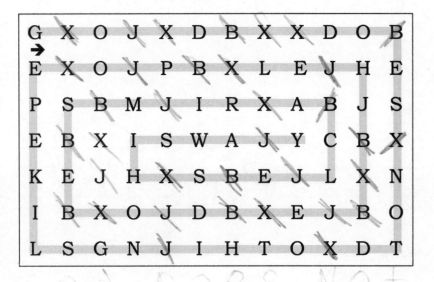

```
G X O J X D B X X D O B
E X O J P B X L E J H E
P S B M J I R X A B J S
E B X I S W A J Y C B X
K E J H X S B E J L X N
I B X O J D B X E J B O
L S G N J I H T O X D T
```

___ ____ ___
__ _____
____ _____.
__ _____
M R P I C A T S
___ ___.

About the Authors

AUTHOR CHRIS BRACK
loves to read all kinds of books, especially kids' books. She, her husband, and her sons share their house with Copper, a basset hound, and Ollie, a huge tomcat.

AUTHOR SHEILA SEIFERT
is an award-winning coauthor of many books, such as *Bible Kidventures: Stories of Danger and Courage*. She likes to find good books for kids to read. Parents can find her bimonthly book flyer at http://simpleliterature.com/bookclub/.

THE KEY TO ADVENTURE LIES WITHIN YOUR IMAGINATION.

OVER **1 MILLION** SOLD IN SERIES

············· **COLLECT ALL OF THEM TODAY!** ·············

AVAILABLE AT A CHRISTIAN RETAILER NEAR YOU

WWW.TYNDALE.COM

CP0874